USBORNE FIRST READING
Level Four

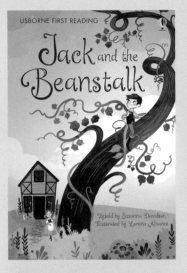

Jack and the Beanstalk
Retold by Susanna Davidson
Illustrated by Lorena Alvarez

Snow White and the Seven Dwarfs
Retold by Lesley Sims
Illustrated by John Joven

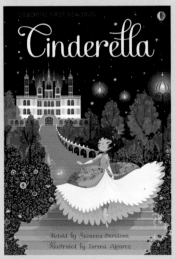

Cinderella
Retold by Susanna Davidson
Illustrated by Lorena Alvarez

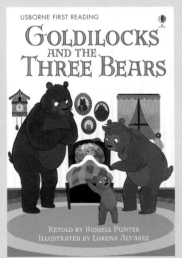

GOLDILOCKS AND THE THREE BEARS
RETOLD BY RUSSELL PUNTER
ILLUSTRATED BY LORENA ALVAREZ

Little Red Riding Hood

Retold by Rob Lloyd Jones

Illustrated by Lorena Alvarez

Reading consultant: Alison Kelly

Once upon a time, there was a girl called Little Red Riding Hood.

Everyone called her Little
Red Riding Hood because that
was what she always wore.

She lived in a creaky house in a creaky forest. Her mother kept bees and made honey.

Her father was a
woodcutter in the forest.

One day, Little Red Riding Hood's mother gave her a pot of honey.

It's for your grandmother.

Little Red Riding Hood's grandmother lived in a cottage on the edge of the forest.

Little Red Riding Hood's house

N

Grandmother's cottage

Little Red Riding Hood put on her red riding hood, and set off.

She skipped along the path, singing a song about her red riding hood.

It's long, it's red, the hood goes on my head, tra la la laa...

"Hello Little Red Riding Hood," called her father.

But someone else was watching Little Red Riding Hood too...

A wolf!
The wolf was hungry.
"I'm fed up of eating bugs
and berries," he moaned.

I want something
bigger in my belly.

As he watched Little Red
Riding Hood, his tummy
rumbled.

He could have just gobbled her up. But the wolf loved making traps.

Quickly, he made a net.

Then he rushed ahead and
laid his trap.

He hid behind a tree and
waited. Little Red Riding
Hood skipped closer...

A hood is good for walking
in the woods, tra la la laa...

She skipped right over
the trap.

"Bother," the wolf muttered.

He scampered from behind the tree, and poked the trap with his paw.

The trap finally worked.

"Bother," the wolf snarled.

The wolf thought of a better
trap. He dug a deep hole and
covered it with sticks. Then
he hid again.

Little Red Riding Hood
skipped closer...

Coats are fine, but if you really want
to shine, wear a hood. Tra la la laa...

She skipped right over
the hole.

"Bother!" the wolf cursed.

He scurried from his hiding place and prodded the sticks with a claw.

WHAAAA!

"Bother!" the wolf cried.

The wolf was too tired
to make another trap.

"I'll just pounce on her and
gobble her up," he decided.

He dashed ahead and hid
again. Little Red Riding
Hood skipped closer.

The wolf pounced...

OOOF!

...and bashed
into the honey pot.

Finally, Little Red Riding Hood saw the wolf. "What a cute little doggy," she said.

"Goodbye doggy," Little Red Riding Hood said. "I'm going to visit my grandma."

The wolf grinned wolfishly. Maybe he could still trick Little Red Riding Hood.

The wolf raced to
Grandma's cottage and
knocked on the door.

Knock!

Knock!

Grandma opened the door...

...and the wolf gobbled her up.

Mmm... bony but tasty.

Quickly he dressed in Grandma's clothes and jumped into her bed.

Now for my brilliant trap.

A minute later there was
another knock on the door.
"Come in," the wolf said,
in a croaky voice.

"I've brought you some honey," said Little Red Riding Hood.

Little Red Riding Hood
looked closely. "Oh
Grandma," she said.
"What big ears you have."

"All the better to hear you
with my dear," said the wolf.

Little Red Riding Hood
came closer. "Oh Grandma,
what big eyes you have."

"All the better to see you
with my dear," said the wolf.

"Oh Grandma," Little Red Riding Hood said. "What big hairy hands you have."

"All the better to hug you with my dear," said the wolf.

Little Red Riding Hood
stepped back. "Oh Grandma,
what big teeth you have."

"All the better to eat you with!" snarled the wolf.

He sprang out of bed and gobbled up Little Red Riding Hood in one bite.

The wolf lay back on the bed. "My trap worked!" He fell into a deep, happy sleep.

In the forest, Little Red Riding Hood's father had finished work.

He decided to go to Grandma's cottage and walk home with Little Red Riding Hood.

There are wolves in these woods, after all.

He reached the cottage and
looked through the window.
There was the wolf, snoring.

"Has that greedy wolf
eaten them both?"

The woodcutter boiled
with fury. Then he had
a brilliant plan of his own.

ZZZZZZZZ

He smashed open the
cottage door.

CRASH!

And he cut open the wolf's
tummy.

Little Red Riding Hood and Grandma tumbled out of the wolf.

Are you all right?

Now Grandma had a brilliant plan too. Chuckling to herself, she ran outside and collected lots of stones.

Little Red Riding Hood
tipped them into the wolf's
tummy, and Grandma sewed
the tummy up.

The wolf woke up and
saw what had happened.
"BOTHER!" he howled.

Rattle
Rattle

The stones rattled with
each step. "Now I'll never be
able to sneak up on anyone."

45

So the wolf went back to eating bugs and berries.

Yuck, a beetle!

And Little Red Riding Hood
skipped all the way home.

About the story

Little Red Riding Hood was first written down around 200 years ago, by brothers Jacob and Wilhelm Grimm. The Grimm brothers, who lived in Germany, collected lots of other classic tales, including *Sleeping Beauty* and *Snow White*.

Designed by Laura Nelson
Series designer: Russell Punter
Series editor: Lesley Sims

First published in 2016 by Usborne Publishing Ltd.,
Usborne House, 83-85 Saffron Hill, London EC1N 8RT, England.
www.usborne.com Copyright © 2016 Usborne Publishing Ltd.

USBORNE FIRST READING
Level Four

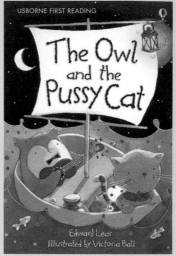

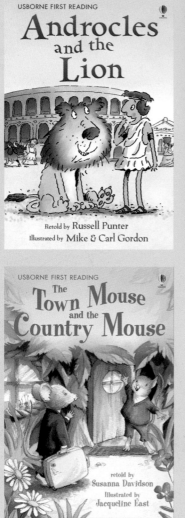